THE BOXCAR CHILDREN® MYSTERIES

THE BOXCAR CHILDREN
SURPRISE ISLAND
THE YELLOW HOUSE MYSTERY
MYSTERY RANCH
MIKE'S MYSTERY
BLUE BAY MYSTERY
THE WOODSHED MYSTERY
THE LIGHTHOUSE MYSTERY
MOUNTAIN TOP MYSTERY
SCHOOLHOUSE MYSTERY
CABOOSE MYSTERY
HOUSEBOAT MYSTERY
SNOWBOUND MYSTERY
TREE HOUSE MYSTERY
BICYCLE MYSTERY
MYSTERY IN THE SAND
MYSTERY BEHIND THE WALL
BUS STATION MYSTERY
BENNY UNCOVERS A MYSTERY
THE HAUNTED CABIN MYSTERY
THE DESERTED LIBRARY MYSTERY
THE ANIMAL SHELTER MYSTERY
THE OLD MOTEL MYSTERY
THE MYSTERY OF THE HIDDEN PAINTING
THE AMUSEMENT PARK MYSTERY
THE MYSTERY OF THE MIXED-UP ZOO
THE CAMP-OUT MYSTERY
THE MYSTERY GIRL
THE MYSTERY CRUISE
THE DISAPPEARING FRIEND MYSTERY
THE MYSTERY OF THE SINGING GHOST
THE MYSTERY IN THE SNOW
THE PIZZA MYSTERY
THE MYSTERY HORSE
THE MYSTERY AT THE DOG SHOW
THE CASTLE MYSTERY
THE MYSTERY OF THE LOST VILLAGE
THE MYSTERY ON THE ICE
THE MYSTERY OF THE PURPLE POOL
THE GHOST SHIP MYSTERY
THE MYSTERY IN WASHINGTON, DC
THE CANOE TRIP MYSTERY
THE MYSTERY OF THE HIDDEN BEACH
THE MYSTERY OF THE MISSING CAT
THE MYSTERY AT SNOWFLAKE INN

THE MYSTERY BOOKSTORE
THE PILGRIM VILLAGE MYSTERY
THE MYSTERY OF THE STOLEN BOXCAR
THE MYSTERY IN THE CAVE
THE MYSTERY ON THE TRAIN
THE MYSTERY AT THE FAIR
THE MYSTERY OF THE LOST MINE
THE GUIDE DOG MYSTERY
THE HURRICANE MYSTERY
THE PET SHOP MYSTERY
THE MYSTERY OF THE SECRET MESSAGE
THE FIREHOUSE MYSTERY
THE MYSTERY IN SAN FRANCISCO
THE NIAGARA FALLS MYSTERY
THE MYSTERY AT THE ALAMO
THE OUTER SPACE MYSTERY
THE SOCCER MYSTERY
THE MYSTERY IN THE OLD ATTIC
THE GROWLING BEAR MYSTERY
THE MYSTERY OF THE LAKE MONSTER
THE MYSTERY AT PEACOCK HALL
THE WINDY CITY MYSTERY
THE BLACK PEARL MYSTERY
THE CEREAL BOX MYSTERY
THE PANTHER MYSTERY
THE MYSTERY OF THE QUEEN'S JEWELS
THE STOLEN SWORD MYSTERY
THE BASKETBALL MYSTERY
THE MOVIE STAR MYSTERY
THE MYSTERY OF THE PIRATE'S MAP
THE GHOST TOWN MYSTERY
THE MYSTERY OF THE BLACK RAVEN
THE MYSTERY IN THE MALL
THE MYSTERY IN NEW YORK
THE GYMNASTICS MYSTERY
THE POISON FROG MYSTERY
THE MYSTERY OF THE EMPTY SAFE
THE HOME RUN MYSTERY
THE GREAT BICYCLE RACE MYSTERY

NOV - - 2021

THE BOXCAR CHILDREN®

CREATED BY
GERTRUDE CHANDLER WARNER

INTERACTIVE
MYSTERY

RACE THROUGH WHITE-WATER CANYON

ILLUSTRATED BY **HOLLIE HIBBERT**

ALBERT WHITMAN & COMPANY
CHICAGO, ILLINOIS

RACE THROUGH
WHITE-WATER CANYON

INTERACTIVE
MYSTERY

CHOOSE A PATH.
FOLLOW THE CLUES.
SOLVE THE MYSTERY!

Can you help the Boxcar Children crack the case? Follow the directions at the end of each section to decide what the Aldens do next. But beware—some routes will end the story before the case is solved. After you finish one path, go back and follow the other paths to see how it all turns out!

SETTING OUT

"Well, what do you know? We made it!" Grandfather Alden exclaimed.

Fourteen-year-old Henry looked out the window just in time to see a wooden welcome sign whiz by. It read, "Welcome to Hemlock, Washington. Population: 51,201."

Henry's younger brother, Benny, pushed his nose up the glass. He was six and was getting antsy after the long drive from the airport. "Can I roll down the window?" he asked.

"Good idea," said Grandfather. "I'll bet these trees smell wonderful!"

Benny rolled down his window, and on the other side of the car, his ten-year-old sister, Violet, rolled hers down too. A rush of warm August air blew through the vehicle. The smell of evergreen trees filled the children's noses.

Jessie took a deep breath and looked up from the map she'd been reading. At twelve, she was the second oldest of the Alden children. She liked to pay attention to the details of their trips. "I wonder if that is why the town is named Hemlock," she said. "Because of the hemlock trees."

"I reckon so," Grandfather said from the driver's seat.

"Are these all hemlocks?" Benny asked, looking out at the rows of tall green trees lining the road.

"Not all of them," said Henry. He'd learned a lot about trees this year in his outdoor adventures after-school club. "But many are. Spruce and fir and pine too."

The fresh air reminded Benny of the time he and his siblings had spent in the forest. After their parents had died, the children had run away. They'd found an abandoned boxcar in a forest and made it their home. That was before Grandfather found them and brought them to live with him in the town of Greenfield, Connecticut.

Benny loved living with Grandfather, but he'd also loved all of the adventures the children had had in the boxcar. He hoped they would find another adventure now, all the way on the other side of the country.

It wasn't long before the car turned onto a street lined with shops. Hemlock was a small town, and that reminded Benny of Greenfield. But instead of having maples and birches along the street, Hemlock was decorated with the same evergreens they'd seen on the drive in.

Grandfather pulled up to a building that looked like an old log cabin. He parked the car under a sign with the name HEMLOCK TOURS hand-painted in bright yellow letters.

As the Aldens were getting out of the car, a man about Grandfather's age came out from the cabin and waved. He had short black hair and a big smile. He was wearing a red plaid shirt and brown fishing pants.

"James Alden!" the man said. He gave Grandfather a big hug. Then he adjusted his round spectacles and looked over the children. "And these must be your grandchildren."

"Yes. This is Henry, Jessie, Violet, and Benny. Children, this is my old friend, Jacob Sully. We met many years ago in college. He owns and runs Hemlock Tours with his daughter, Elizabeth. She's the one who will be leading your tour."

"She goes by Liz now," Jacob said, winking over his spectacles. "Nice to meet you, kids. And welcome to Hemlock. Ready for the best three days of your lives?"

"Am I ever!" said Benny. The Aldens had spent weeks planning their river-rafting trip. After so much waiting, Benny couldn't wait to get started.

Jacob opened the door to the cabin. The inside was friendly and comfortable with a fireplace and a few big, comfy couches. All across the walls were hiking, rafting, and fishing gear: life vests, fishing rods, kayaks, and many other knickknacks. A big map of Washington State hung in the middle of the wall, marked with the many places visitors could go on tours.

A woman with the same black hair and big smile as Jacob was sitting in a log armchair, tightening the laces on her waterproof boots. She stood up as the Aldens arrived.

"This is my daughter, Liz. She leads the rafting and hiking tours," Jacob explained. "Liz, these are the Aldens: Henry, Jessie, Violet, and Benny."

"What a great crew! I can already tell we're going to have a great time," Liz said cheerfully. "Have any of you ever gone white-water rafting before?"

"We've been on lots of kinds of boats, but this will be our first time rafting," Henry said.

"Perfect! It's toward the end of the season, so the water level will be lower. That means plenty of exciting rapids. But there are also fewer visitors, so we'll be able to take our time."

"Is it more dangerous at this time of year?" Violet asked.

"It can be," Liz replied. "But don't you worry. I'll make sure you all know your way around the gear and the rapids. I promise, over the next few days, you'll have the best tour in the Pacific Northwest."

"If you're all set, you should get going," Jacob said. "While you're on your white-water adventure, your grandfather and I will be having a much more easygoing time—fly fishing."

"Isn't that the kind where you stand in the river all day?" Benny asked.

Jacob nodded. "That's right."

"That sounds boring," said Benny.

Grandfather chuckled. "Yes. It's very boring, and that's precisely why I love it. You'll understand one day when you're older."

Benny wasn't so sure about that. But he was happy Grandfather would be doing something he liked while they were on their rafting tour.

"If you're ready to head out, I have a pack prepared for each of you," Liz said. She gestured toward the door where four hiking packs were waiting on a bench. Liz already had her pack slung over her shoulder.

"These are heavy. What's inside?" Benny asked.

"Everything we'll need for our trip," Liz said. She grinned. "Think you can handle it?"

Benny shouldered the pack. He tipped over a little bit from the weight but then stood up straight. "I sure can!"

The children said good-bye to Grandfather and

took their packs. Then they followed Liz outside.

"You can load your things in my truck," Liz said, pointing up the street. "The green one that says *Hemlock Tours* on it. Dad likes me to park it on the corner because he says it's good advertising."

"Are there a lot of tours out of Hemlock?" Henry asked.

"Oh yes. We have quite a bit of competition," Liz said. "But I like to think we stand out above the rest."

As the group walked, loud music blasted from a truck behind them. They were about to cross the street when Liz grabbed Benny and pulled him back.

"Look out!"

It was just in time. A blue pickup turned in front of them, speeding through the crosswalk. On the side of the truck were the words *Bandit River Tours*. The truck sped away.

"Speaking of competition..." Liz grumbled. "Anyways, come on. Here's my truck."

The Aldens helped Liz load up the gear before climbing inside. It was a tight squeeze, but Liz assured them it wasn't a long ride.

"That truck said 'Bandit River,'" Violet said. "Is that the name of a river around here? I didn't see it on Jessie's map."

Liz sighed. She drove the truck down a curvy road. Luckily the truck's big tires seemed well equipped to navigate the way, and Liz did not seem worried. "The real name is Hemlock River. But some folks in town call it Bandit River after...let's call it a local legend," Liz said.

Before Violet could ask more about Bandit River, the trees cleared, and the view took her breath away. A wide stretch of blue water flowed in front of them, sparkling in the afternoon sun. The road ended at a parking lot and a long boat dock.

Several trucks and cars were parked near the dock, including the Bandit River Tours truck. As Liz parked, a man with a green bandanna tied around his forehead got out, followed by a young couple who started taking pictures with their phones.

"This is the bottom of Sixth Street," said the bandanna-wearing tour guide. "Here you'll see the lamppost that went out on the night Fred Feriston made his escape."

The couple started taking photos of the lamppost at the corner of the parking lot.

"It doesn't look very special to me," Henry said.

"It's not, but people will still pay top dollar to take a photo of it," Liz muttered.

"Hey, Liz!" the other tour guide called, louder than was necessary. "How's it going? Seen any cool trees today?" The last part sounded especially unnecessary.

"It's going fine, Jonny. No cool trees today. How are you?" Liz called back, though Jessie didn't think she sounded like she really wanted to know.

The guide for Bandit River Tours leaned on his truck and gave a grin. "Oh, you know. Business is booming. My inbox is overflowing. The spirit of Fred Feriston is alive and well. I'm glad to see you got at least one tour booked before the end of the season," he said, flashing a competitive smile.

Jessie could tell that Liz and Jonny did not get along. "Just ignore him," she suggested.

"Good idea," Liz agreed, turning her back on Jonny and smiling to the Aldens. Together they

unloaded the truck and chatted as they made their way down to the river.

Their raft was waiting for them on the side of the dock. It was a bright yellow color, the same shade as the letters on the sign of the Hemlock Tours cabin. While Liz loaded up the gear, they could hear Jonny talking to his tour group.

"He doesn't seem like he means well," Jessie said. "Was that a joke—about cool trees?"

"Jonny and I did our white-water training together," Liz said. "He wasn't always like this. But when he took over his family's tour business and turned it into the Bandit River thing, he got obsessed with making money and getting likes on his social media account. He's always making fun of me because I have a degree in arboriculture."

"What's that?" Benny asked.

"Basically...it's a degree in trees," said Liz.

"I think that's really interesting," said Henry.

"Thanks," Liz said, trying to cheer up. "Jonny thinks a lot of the stuff I talk about on tours is boring. All he wants to tell his tours about is Fred Feriston."

"Is that part of the local legend you were talking

about?" Henry asked. "I think I saw a sign with his name on it in town."

"Is he the bandit of Bandit River?" Benny asked.

Liz nodded. "Yes. I don't know all the details because it's mostly just a legend. You know how sometimes things happen, but they grow and get more exaggerated when people tell the story over and over again?" she asked.

Benny said, "Like the stories Grandfather tells about the fish he catches?"

Liz laughed. "Yes, I suppose it's a little like that. But sometimes people exaggerate for reasons that aren't so innocent."

Jessie glanced over her shoulder at Jonny and his tour group. "Like when it means making more money off of tours?" she asked.

"Exactly," Liz said as she strapped their gear into the raft. "The story goes that twenty years ago, a man named Fred Feriston showed up in Hemlock and got a job as a tour guide at a rafting company. At first he was quiet and didn't talk much, but everyone loved him because he was so hardworking and knowledgeable about the river.

Then when he started to get to know people, he began talking about his grandmother, who he said was very sick. Over the summer that he led the tours, tourists and townspeople alike donated money to help him and his grandmother. Five thousand dollars in one summer. But then, right at the end of the season, the story goes that he took the money and just...vanished."

"Why did he leave without telling anyone?" Violet asked with a frown.

"No one knows," said Liz. "But people say he took the money for himself—that he was a thief who went from town to town, leaving without a trace each time."

"How dishonest," said Henry. "Now I get why people would call him a bandit."

Liz finished strapping their packs into the raft. "Yes, the name makes sense, but I always thought there was more to the story. Unfortunately, Jonny and the others at Bandit River Tours don't seem interested in finding the rest out."

All the talk of money and a vanishing bandit had gotten Benny's attention. "Do you think there might be clues about where he went? Maybe we can solve the mystery of Bandit River!" he said.

Liz laughed. "I guess it's possible, but don't get your hopes up. It's been twenty years. And we don't even know if all the parts of the legend are true. But you know what? Enough about Jonny and his tour! This raft is set to go. Are you ready to start *our* adventure?"

The four children listened as Liz explained how to stay safe while they were on the rapids. Violet, in particular, listened closely. She was a little nervous about the raft and wanted to make sure she knew what to do if there were problems. Luckily, Liz was very good at explaining.

After Liz was done talking, the group pushed the yellow raft into the water alongside the dock. Then, on the count of three, they pushed off and jumped in. A moment later they were bobbing along on the rippling current of Hemlock River.

Jessie and Violet sat on the right side of the raft, and Henry and Benny sat on the left. It took a little while to get used to paddling as a group, but with Liz's instructions, soon the crew of five was easily navigating the winding river.

At one turn, the current pulled them into a swirling eddy, and water splashed over the front of the raft. Violet moved to the center of the raft to make sure she wouldn't fall out. But after a couple more rough patches, she got used to paddling through the bumps and started to enjoy the cool splashes of water.

"All right, kids, the river is about to split," Liz said after a while. "We're going left, down the scenic route. It's good for beginners."

"What's to the right?" Benny asked.

"That way is the white-water rapids," answered Liz. "It's pretty challenging, especially this time of year."

Just then a streak of red flashed by them on the river. The Aldens watched as a woman in a bright red kayak steered through the frothy water ahead, her paddle flipping in and out of the water like a fish's fins. The kayak shot ahead as the split in the river approached and darted to the right.

"That looks awesome!" Benny exclaimed. "Let's

follow her!"

"It does look like fun," said Henry.

"Do you think we're ready for rapids?" Violet asked Liz. She was feeling better in the raft, but she wasn't so sure she was ready for rapids.

"I'll leave that up to you," said Liz. "But we have to decide now. Left or right?"

IF THE ALDENS FOLLOW THE RED KAYAK TO THE RIGHT, GO TO PAGE 17.

IF THE CHILDREN TAKE THE LONG WAY TO THE LEFT, GO TO PAGE 24.

WHITE-WATER RIDE

"Come on, Violet. It looks like fun!" Benny said.

Violet watched the woman in the red kayak zip through the rapids. The white water sprayed up and glittered in the sun. It did look exciting.

"Okay, let's go!" she shouted.

Liz's hesitation disappeared when she saw how eager the Alden children were to take on the rapids. She grinned.

"All right, then. Hold on tight, and do as I tell you!" she said.

Liz steered the raft to the right. As soon as they got to the part of the river where the woman in the red kayak had been, the water picked up speed. It seemed like the raft was being pulled ahead by an invisible rope.

"Remember, kids, if you fall out, all you need to do is lift up your legs and float downstream. Your life vest will keep you safe. The important thing is to stay calm and aware of your surroundings. Got it?"

"Aye, aye, captain!" Benny cheered.

Cool droplets sprayed up from the river as the Aldens approached the rapids. The children worked hard to help Liz steer, plunging their paddles deep into the water with each command she yelled out.

When she said, "Forward paddle!" they paddled as hard and fast as they could. When she said, "Everyone left!" everyone went to the left side of the raft to avoid scraping over a rock. When she said, "Hold on!" through a rough patch, they all grabbed onto the rope that lined the edge of the raft to keep from falling out.

And when she suddenly shouted, "Everyone down!" they all moved to the center of the raft and held their paddles out of the water. As they did, the raft bounced on a big wave and lifted off the water for a moment. Then *FOOM!* the raft lurched down like a roller coaster.

"Back on the job," Liz called, as the Aldens took their places back on both sides of the raft. She had a big grin on her face. "You're doing great!"

Violet could feel her heart pounding and river water on her cheeks. She realized she was grinning too. Her nervousness had turned to excitement.

They followed Liz's commands and worked their way down the rapids. The raft bounced against rocks that seemed to pop out of the water. Sometimes the rocks were invisible until the last second, when the water would slosh away and reveal them. But Liz was an expert guide, and even though the children had never been rafting on white water, they had been on a lot of other adventures, and they were excellent listeners.

When Violet looked up, she could see the end of the rapids, where the other branch of the river rejoined the route they were on. They were almost through!

Suddenly, Violet felt her paddle jerk backward. Rocks had come up alongside the raft, and her paddle had gotten wedged in a crack. She lost her grip on the paddle. As she reached for it, the raft lurched and bounced, and that was it. Violet fell into the water with a big, cold splash.

"Oh no!" Jessie cried. She grabbed for her sister, but Violet was underwater.

Violet spit out water when she surfaced. With her life vest keeping her afloat, she was able to swim to the rock where her paddle was stuck.

Liz and Henry managed to paddle the raft to the side of the river, where Liz grabbed onto a fallen tree sticking out over the water.

"Don't worry about the paddle," Liz shouted to Violet. "Let go of the rock and float toward us."

Violet looked toward the raft. If she let go of the rock, she could float right toward them. But she didn't want to give up her paddle. If she didn't have it, she couldn't help steer the raft.

"I've almost got it," she said, pulling herself up, out of the spray of the water.

She yanked on the paddle, but just as it came free, it slipped out of her hands. In a flash it was zipping downriver with the current.

"Well, there goes that idea," Violet said to herself. She glanced to where her siblings and Liz were trying to keep the raft close to shore. She knew that Liz had told her to lift up her feet and float down the river if she fell out, but now that she was holding on to the rock, she was finding it hard to let go.

"I don't know if I can do it," she called.

"Don't worry, Violet," Henry called back. "We're coming for you."

Violet sat on the rock while Liz tied the raft off to a branch on the fallen tree. Henry and Jessie were the first ones out and ran up the shore. Henry waded into the rapids to help. It took a little effort, but soon Violet was back on land.

"It's okay. I've got you," Henry said.

Violet walked back to the raft with Henry and Jessie. Liz and Benny were waiting on the shore next to where the raft was tied up.

"Whew!" Liz exclaimed. "That was pretty exciting. You doing okay, Violet?"

Violet nodded. "Just a little wet. Well, a lot wet. But I'm okay."

"Good, I'm glad you're all right. We'll wait just a minute so you can catch your breath. Does anyone want a snack?"

"I do!" Benny said.

Liz grabbed the food pack out of the raft and opened it. Just as she was taking out a few granola bars, a commotion came from up the river. A blue raft came careening down the rapids. In it were Jonny and his tour group. Jonny cheered loudly as they approached, and sprays of water flew as he paddled. Jessie thought he looked a little out of control, and his raft was headed right for the place where the Aldens' raft was tied up.

"Whoa!" Liz shouted, waving her arm. "Can't you see us? Left turn. Left!"

Jonny saw Liz and their raft at the last second. He shouted, "Left turn!" but it was too late. His blue raft smashed right into Liz's yellow one. The tree branch that held the raft's mooring line snapped. Liz tried to grab the rope but missed. Their raft headed downstream without them.

"Sorry!" Jonny called as he and his rafters sped away.

"He didn't sound sorry," said Jessie.

Liz let out a frustrated grumble. She took out her phone and started texting. "I'll let the dock downriver know to expect our raft. As for us, I'm afraid we have a bit of a hike before we can get started again. My dad and your grandfather already left for their fishing trip, so there's no one to bring us a second raft. Looks like our white-water adventure is over for now."

Jessie sighed. "I guess it can't be helped."

"Look on the bright side," said Henry. "At least we're all safe."

"Not just that," added Benny. He held up a granola bar. "The snacks are safe too!"

THE END

TO FOLLOW A DIFFERENT PATH, GO TO PAGE 16.

LONG WAY ROUND

Jessie noticed Liz and Violet's hesitation.

"I think it'll be safer for us to take the easier way this time," she said. "We can warm up to the tough rapids."

"Jessie's right," said Henry. "Let's take the scenic route."

The group paddled to the left, where the river widened, and the water became calmer and smoother. It took only the occasional paddle from Liz to keep the raft on course, so the children were able to put down their paddles and enjoy the scenery.

On both banks of the river, tall trees rose up out of the gray stone. Henry noticed that most of them were hemlock and cedar trees, with boughs full of silvery-green needles and pinecones. The water was clear enough to see minnows flitting about in big schools just under the raft. Benny even spotted a friendly river otter playing on a fallen tree.

"Well, would you look at that," Liz said, pointing.

Above them a big bird soared, casting a shadow that rippled across the calm water. Jessie looked closer at its brown body, broad wings, and white head.

"A bald eagle!" she said.

"Yep," Liz said, smiling up at it. "When I was Benny's age, bald eagles were an endangered species. But they've made a great comeback, thanks to better protections. Now we see them almost all year long."

"Can I take a picture of it?" Violet asked.

"Sure. The water will stay nice and calm, so it should be safe for you to take out your camera," Liz said.

Violet reached into one of the waterproof packs and pulled out her digital camera. The Aldens took turns taking photos while Liz steered from the back of the raft.

"This is beautiful," Violet said.

"Yeah," said Benny. But he sounded a little disappointed.

"I know you wanted to go on the white-water rapids," Jessie said, "but I think we need a little more practice first." She ruffled Benny's hair playfully.

"The rapids will always be there when you're ready," Liz agreed. "And anyway, if we had gone on the rapids, we would have missed something just as cool. Look up ahead."

The sound of rushing water rose over the sound of singing bugs and birds. The river turned and widened into a big pool. Up above, pouring from blue and gray rocks, was a waterfall.

Liz brought the raft to the bank.

"It's not just for looking at, Benny," Liz said. "The water's nice and deep here, and there are no rocks at the bottom. Do you know what that means?" She pointed up at a rocky ledge above them, which stuck out next to the waterfall.

Benny's eyes lit up. "We can jump?" he asked. He looked at Henry and Jessie. "Can I? Please?"

Jessie laughed. "Of course!" she said. "As long as you keep your life jacket on!"

Liz showed them the trail that led to the ledge next to the waterfall. There were a few places to jump off of into the pool below. At first Benny was excited, but when he got to the edge and looked down, he wasn't so sure. It looked higher up from the top.

"I'll go with you," Henry said. "Ready? On three!"

"One, two, three!" Benny counted, and they jumped in with a big splash.

While Henry, Jessie, and Benny jumped into the water, Violet explored closer to the waterfall. At the base the rocks were slippery with spray from the falls. Water gathered in pools full of pebbles and bright green moss. Violet noticed some purple flowers next to the falls and took out her camera. But as she looked through the viewfinder, she saw something move quickly to the side.

A shiny creature about three times the size of Violet's hand was sitting in a pool of water near where the falls splashed over the side of the rocks. It looked like a lizard, with a long brown body covered in dark brown spots. It had big eyes, and it stared at her from a bed of moss.

Violet quietly turned to take a picture of the creature.

"Look out below!" cried Benny from above. At the sound of Benny splashing into the water, the creature twitched, then it scurried into the shadows behind the falls.

"It's okay, don't be scared," Violet said, but the creature didn't come back out. So Violet lowered her camera and edged along the rocks behind the falls. "I've never seen a critter like you before. Will you come out long enough for me to take your picture?" she called.

She discovered that there wasn't just rock behind the waterfall. There was a cave. Inside, the afternoon sunshine shone through the water and created a light show on the gray stone. Emerald moss hung from the rocks, dripping with water.

The lizard-like creature was sitting on a flat, shiny rock, watching Violet. Careful not to frighten the animal, Violet raised her camera. She managed to take a photo before the little thing

got nervous and disappeared into a hole in the rocks. Violet put her camera down, happy she'd gotten at least one picture.

Just then she noticed that the rock the creature had been sitting on wasn't a rock at all. It looked like a piece of plastic.

"Did someone leave garbage back here?" Violet asked out loud. She took the thing in her hand and found it was a plastic bag with a rectangle inside. "No, not garbage...a book?"

Violet came out from behind the waterfall. Her siblings were waiting.

"Where'd you go?" Benny asked.

"And what did you find?" Jessie added.

"I saw a neat-looking lizard and went to take its picture. When I went back there, I found this," Violet explained. She opened the bag. Inside was an old book. She handed it to Henry, who looked it over. Next, she showed the picture she'd taken to Liz.

"Do you know what this is?" she asked.

Liz's eyes grew when she saw the picture. "You bet I do. That's a Pacific giant salamander! They're extremely rare to find. I'd say you could take it as a good luck sign that you were able to get such a wonderful picture!" she said.

"This book seems to be a journal. The name in the front says Christopher Francis," Henry said. He showed them the name written on the front page. "Does that ring any bells for you, Liz?"

"Not me," Liz said. "A bit mysterious that they would stow a book in such a place though."

"Mysterious? Maybe it's a clue to the Bandit River mystery!" Benny said hopefully.

Jessie laughed. "It would really make your day if it were, wouldn't it, Benny?" she teased.

"Yes. You know what else would make my day?" Benny asked. "Jumping from the waterfall again!"

CONTINUE TO PAGE 32

WHITE-RIVER FALLS

The Aldens stayed at the waterfall for an hour or so before returning to the raft and heading down the river. The current was still easygoing enough that Liz said she could handle it on her own. When she said it, though, she sounded tired.

"Are you sure? Why don't you let me row for a bit," Henry suggested. At first Liz hesitated, but then she nodded and put down her paddle.

"Thanks, Henry," she said. "I guess a rest could be nice."

"You've been doing a lot of the work while we've been learning," said Henry. "I'm glad to help now that I'm more comfortable."

Henry went to the back of the raft to steer, and Liz joined the others.

"Has it been a busy season?" asked Jessie.

Liz sighed. "It has been for me. We had to let go of our other guide last year because we weren't getting as much business, so I have been leading all of the tours this year."

"What happened?" asked Jessie.

"Well, it used to be that we got a lot of business from people wanting to go on hikes and rafting tours. But the last couple years, things have changed. People don't seem as interested in our tour, which is more focused on nature. More and more people want to go on the tour that focuses on the river bandit."

"I'm sorry to hear that," Henry said.

"Me too. I've always done tours the way my dad taught me, you know? Trees and rivers and Pacific giant salamanders are what made me fall in love with Hemlock River. But I guess maybe that's not enough for some people."

"Well, I think you're a great guide," said Violet. "Those people don't know what they're missing. I'm sure things will turn around for you and your father."

"Thanks, Violet. I sure hope so," Liz said.

Jessie broke out the snacks, and everyone munched on trail mix and granola bars as they continued down the river. Violet wanted to look through the journal she'd found, but she didn't want to accidentally drop it over the side of the raft. So, instead, she kept it stowed in her pack. Maybe she would have a chance to look at it more closely when they reached their destination for the night.

The sky changed from a bright blue to a pink-peach as the sun began to set. Liz was back to steering the raft, and she turned the raft toward shore, where a dock had come into view. The sign on the dock read, "Welcome to White-River Falls." Just off the dock, a road led up to a small town. Beyond the town was a thick forest, which covered the mountains above like a green blanket.

"We made it!" Liz said. "Our first night's stop."

The children helped Liz unload the raft and pull it out of the water. There were a few other people at the dock too. One of them, Jessie recognized, was the woman from the red kayak, who had passed them on the river. She was sitting on a tree stump sipping a tin cup of coffee. Her short, straight hair hung down from a wrinkled fishing cap, and she nodded at Jessie when their eyes met.

Farther down the dock, Jonny was working to get his tour group out of the water. From the looks of it, they had gone through the rapids and taken a dunk in the river. All three of them were soaking wet, and the young couple didn't look happy about it.

"My phone is all wet. It won't turn on," complained the young woman. "I hope this is covered by your insurance."

"Let's just get to the hotel and into some dry clothes," said the young man. The two stormed away, leaving Jonny to finish with the raft. He grumbled to himself while he worked. Then, after a minute, he stopped grumbling and started whistling to himself instead.

"Are we staying at a hotel too?" Benny asked.

"Yep, the same one they're staying at," Liz said. "Unless, that is, you want to rough it in the woods!" She made a hand like a bear claw and grinned.

"Yeah!" Benny started to say, but Jessie shook her head no. "I mean, no. A hotel is fine."

"When we get there, we can look through that journal Violet found behind the waterfall," Henry said.

Benny lit up. "I wonder if it has any clues about Fred Feriston!"

Benny spoke so loudly the woman sitting on the stump and another tour looked over at them.

Jonny finished with his raft and came over, wringing the water out of his bandanna as he walked. "Fred Feriston, you say?"

"Mind your own business, Jonny," Liz said.

"I am minding my own business. And that business has everything to do with Fred Feriston. You see, kids, my family owns the Fred Feriston museum here in White-River Falls. The only museum all about Fred Feriston, in fact. And even though you're not on my Bandit River tour, I'd be willing to let you visit for free."

"And why is that?" Liz asked.

"Because the more the merrier, Liz," Jonny said, flashing a smile. He turned back to the

Aldens. "Anyway, once you see the museum, I'm sure you'll want to hear everything there is to know about Fred Feriston. And Liz here might be great at dodging rocks in white-water rapids, but there's only one guy in the Hemlock area who can tell you all the Bandit River information you want to know."

Jonny pointed at his chest.

Liz stood up and brushed off her hands. She'd finished tying up the raft.

"I was going to take the Aldens on a hike up to the old sawmill," she said. "Though we did get in a little later than I expected."

"What? The sawmill is boring. Anyway, you look tired. Why don't you take a load off? Get some coffee; relax with Maggie." Jonny motioned toward the woman sitting on the stump. "Trust me to entertain your tour for a bit."

Liz turned to the children to discuss. "I just love the sawmill, and we still have time for a visit," she said. "But part of being a good guide is listening to what your group wants. I may not be a big fan of Jonny, but it's no problem with me if you want to go to the museum. I'm okay relaxing for a bit."

Henry turned to his siblings. "What do you think?"

**IF THE ALDENS GO TO THE SAWMILL,
GO TO PAGE 39.**

**IF THE ALDENS GO TO THE MUSEUM,
GO TO PAGE 47.**

JOURNEY TO THE SAWMILL

"I'd like to stick with Liz and her tour plan," said Jessie, "if it's all the same to everyone else." She didn't say so, but Jessie didn't really trust Jonny, even if she usually enjoyed visiting museums.

"The sawmill hike sounds like good exercise," said Henry. "And I want to see what it looks like."

Violet and Benny nodded in agreement.

"Maybe we'll visit the museum another time," Jessie told Jonny.

"All right, but if you get bored out in the woods, you know where to find me," he said. He gave one of his grins, tipped an invisible hat, and then strolled toward town.

Liz looked relieved. "I'm glad. I really enjoy the hike, so I was hoping I could show you. It's a traditional part of my father's old tours and an important part of understanding Hemlock history. But we should get moving. The sun will be down soon," she said.

"Lead the way!" said Jessie.

The Aldens' arms were tired from rowing, but their legs still had plenty of energy. To save time they left their packs stowed underneath their raft and followed Liz away from the dock. She led them to a narrow walking trail along the shoreline. Although the trail was clear enough, it didn't seem like too many people used it. In some places branches grew into the open space, and in others the children had to climb over fallen trees.

After a ways, the trail bent away from the shoreline into the thick woods that bordered the river on either side. Benny looked up at the sky.

"It's sure getting dark fast," he said.

"Yep," Liz said. "Out here there aren't many city lights, so the stars really show. We're even able to see the northern lights sometimes in the winter." She glanced over her shoulder and smiled. "What do you know about forests, Benny?"

Benny thought for a moment. "Well, I know they're full of trees. And there are lots of animals that live there. But some places have different animals. Like in the rain forest they have animals like leopards and orangutans." Benny looked around the forest. He didn't know what kinds of animals lived in Washington. "Are there orangutans in this kind of forest!"

Liz turned to him. "No, none of those. But there are foxes and owls and deer and bears. Higher up in the mountains, there are elk and mountain goats."

Benny stopped so suddenly Violet bumped into him.

"Bears?" he asked. He had thought Liz was kidding when she'd made a claw sign at him by the dock. "Are there really bears here?"

Liz gave him her biggest smile. "They almost never come this close to town. And tomorrow night we'll be sure to hang our food packs up when we're camping. Usually when I've come across a bear, it's after the beef jerky my dad likes to bring along."

This made Benny feel better. Still, he kept his eyes peeled as they walked.

After a little while, the footpath joined a road leading up a hill. The road was wide enough for a truck, but it too looked like it hadn't been used in a long time. At the top of the hill stood a large wooden structure with a tin roof. It was shaped like an apartment building or a hotel, but once the children were inside, they saw that it was different from any other place they'd been.

The inside was wide open all the way up to the rafters. Huge pieces of equipment towered before them. Long conveyer belts stretched the length of the building, and at the end of the belts were tall metal blades.

"Welcome to the White-River Sawmill," Liz said, putting her hands on her hips. "This sawmill was in use until about twenty years ago. It was about that time when all the logging got taken up by bigger companies. But it's preserved here as a historical landmark."

"The saw blades are huge," Henry said. He examined a loose blade on a table, but he kept his distance.

"They look dangerous," Violet said. Even though

it was clear none of the saws had been used in many years, she could imagine the deafening sound they'd made when they had been used to split trees.

"It was dangerous," Liz agreed. "Logging in general is very dangerous work, especially back when this mill was in use. There was the risk of trees falling out of control and logs rolling off of a truck. Here in the sawmill, accidents happened as well. In fact, the reason this mill ended up closing was because a man named James Green got hurt while he was on the job."

Violet took pictures while Liz spoke. It was a bit of a challenge in the dim light, but she still managed to get some good shots with her flash on.

"After his injury, Mr. Green stood up to the logging companies for their poor working conditions," Liz continued. "Of course, the logging companies weren't happy about that, especially when it hurt their business. Still, many people look up to Mr. Green for speaking up for workers. There's even a statue of him back in town. I'll show you when we get back. Speaking of...We should probably head out. It's getting dark."

The children took one last look at the spooky, old sawmill before following Liz back outside. They were glad they had come. It was amazing to think that the green forest they'd just walked through had once been full of logging equipment and workers.

Outside, the stars were already coming out, and the only light was from the half-moon in the sky above. Benny kept his eyes extra peeled for dangerous animals on the way back, but Liz made him feel better. She knew the way and whistled cheerfully as they went along.

Eventually the glow of the streetlamps shone through the trees, and the Aldens returned to the dock where they'd left their raft.

"Now let's grab our things and check into the hotel," Liz said.

The children grabbed their packs out from under the raft, but Violet frowned when she picked up hers. The strap holding it closed was undone. When she opened it up and looked inside, she gasped.

"What's wrong?" Jessie asked.

"The journal I found at the falls," Violet said. "It's gone! I know I put it right here. I didn't want it to fall out of the raft into the river. But now I think someone took it!"

The children looked up and down the street, but no one was around. Not the young couple on the Bandit River tour, not Jonny. Not even the woman with the red kayak.

"I'm sorry to say this, Violet," Liz apologized, "but whoever took it is long gone."

Violet sighed. Liz was right.

"Whatever was inside must have been important to someone. But I guess now we won't figure out why," she said.

THE END

TO FOLLOW A DIFFERENT PATH, GO TO PAGE 38.

THE BANDIT RIVER MUSEUM

"I want to learn more about Fred Feriston," Benny said.

"And I think we could all use a bit of a rest," Jessie added.

Liz looked a little disappointed but said, "That's probably for the best. It's getting late."

Henry nodded. "You've worked hard today, and it's only day one of the tour. Take a break, and we'll entertain ourselves for a little while," he said.

Liz nodded. "All right. But at least let me get you checked into the hotel before you go to the museum," she said.

"I'll see you there," Jonny said to the Aldens. He tipped an imaginary hat and walked away with a jaunty whistle.

Race through White-Water Canyon

The children picked up their packs from the raft and followed Liz. It was only a short walk down the main street to their destination. The front of the hotel was old-fashioned, like a lodge built out of red logs. Inside, the main lobby was just as rustic, with red and green carpeting and a chandelier made of antlers.

Liz checked the children in at the desk, and they loaded their packs onto a brass luggage cart. In exchange for the cart, Liz handed them a key card with their room number written on it.

"I'll take these up to the room. After the museum, head on back here, and we'll have some supper. But do me a favor and don't leave Main Street, okay? Cell phone reception is spotty, and it gets really dark out here. It's easy to get lost if you don't know where you're going."

"You got it," Henry said.

"Have a good rest!" Benny added.

The way to the museum was simple. The children followed the main street until they saw an old brick building with a statue in front of it. The statue was of two men shaking hands. One man wore a business suit. The other man was wearing a logger's uniform of heavy overalls and a flannel shirt, and he had an ax resting across his shoulders.

"Wonder what they're shaking hands about," Benny said.

There was a brass plaque at the base of the statue. It was lit by the streetlamps, which were coming on as the sun went down. "Let's read it together," said Jessie.

She helped her little brother sound out the words on the plaque: *James Green: Founder of Forest Friends. You will always have a friend among the loggers of White-River Falls!*

"What's a logger?" Benny asked.

"It's someone whose work is to cut down trees and prepare them as lumber," Henry said. "Logging is how we get all the wood that we use to build things like houses and bridges."

"Like a lumberjack?" Benny asked. "That man does look like a lumberjack!"

Jessie laughed. "Yes, exactly. A lumberjack is just one of the many jobs in the logging business. And he does. He must be James Green. It sounds like he did something important for the workers of White-River Falls."

They heard footsteps approaching. Jonny had seen them reading the plaque and came out from the museum nearby.

"He sure did. Logging is a big business in this area and has been for a very long time. Lots of families who live in White-River Falls and Hemlock have a history with the logging business. So when this guy, James Green, fought for safer working conditions about twenty years ago, it meant a lot to people," he explained.

"What's Forest Friends?" Violet asked.

"That's the name of the organization he started to make logging safer for workers," Jonny said.

"It sounds like a league of superheroes," Benny said. "Did they wear capes and masks?"

Jonny's laugh was big and loud, drawing the attention of the few passersby on the street. Jessie thought he seemed friendlier when he wasn't talking about Bandit River Tours.

"They might as well have worn capes. James Green and the Forest Friends were like superheroes to the people of this area. Not like that bandit Fred Feriston. Speaking of which—come on, I'll show you around the museum," he said, waving them along.

The museum itself had an old feeling to it, just like the hotel and the other buildings in town. It was just a single large room on the inside, with big log rafters holding up the peaked roof. A bright banner hung from the center with the words *Bandit River Museum* on it. The blue of the banner matched the truck that Jonny drove. Under the main title on the banner were the words *Tag us on social media! #fredferistonstolemytour*.

"They're really trying to make money on the whole Fred Feriston bandit thing, aren't they?" Henry said quietly.

Jonny hadn't heard him. He gestured grandly.

"Welcome to the Bandit River Museum." From his tone of voice, the children could tell this was a speech he had given many times. "Here we've stored every bit of information available about the notorious bandit Fred Feriston, who made off with thousands of dollars twenty years ago. After tricking people over the course of a summer, he snuck away in the middle of the night with a bag filled with money that had been given to him by the kind people of Hemlock."

The children followed Jonny to the first exhibit, which was a big map of the Hemlock River. Drawn on it was a red line that showed Fred Feriston's escape route.

"Fred first appeared in the neighboring town of Hemlock, just ten miles upriver. He told everyone he was from White-River Falls, and at first no one questioned it. But after some time, the people of Hemlock started asking about him. Turns out no one in White-River Falls had ever heard of anyone named Fred Feriston...and then, just as mysteriously as he appeared, a few days later, he vanished," Jonny said.

"Did they check the river for clues?" Benny asked. "When we were in Hemlock, you said he used that boat landing to escape. Maybe he dropped something that could help people find him."

"That's why it is such a big mystery. Townsfolk searched for days, up and down the river and in the woods on either bank," Jonny said. "Some people thought he might have washed ashore. After all, on the night of his escape there was a terrible storm, and the river is no place to be at night. But no one could find a trace of him. My father was a sheriff back then and was part of the search party. When he retired, he made this museum to store all the information we've been able to gather over the years."

"*And* so you can get customers for your tours," Henry said.

"Yes. Well, we have to pay the bills somehow," Jonny admitted with a grin.

"I still don't understand how he managed to get so much money," Violet said. "Five thousand dollars is a lot to be donated to someone that no one knew."

Jonny waved them along to a well-lit glass case with sheets of paper tacked on a board. When the children got closer, they could see it was a collection of newspaper clippings and handwritten letters.

"Fred knew what he was doing. He made sure to post in the *Hemlock Daily* about his grandmother, and he even wrote letters to the wealthier folks in town, asking if they could help. The people of Hemlock are a close-knit bunch. They care about each other. In the beginning, Fred seemed friendly and honest, so they were happy to give money to his cause," Jonny said.

Violet looked at the letters Fred had written. Something seemed familiar about them. But she wasn't sure why.

Henry moved on to another display case. Inside was a yellow cap. It had faded over time, but it had probably been very bright at one time.

"What's this?" Henry asked.

"That is the only thing Fred Feriston left behind on the night of his escape," Jonny said. "His bright yellow cap. Eyewitnesses said he was wearing it as he ran through town. But by the time the townsfolk had followed him to the dock, he was gone. This is the only clue anyone's been able to find."

"Until what Violet found behind the waterfall," Benny said.

"Shh," said Violet, but it was too late.

"Oh? What did she find?" Jonny tried to sound

casual, but the children could tell he was very interested.

"It's nothing," Henry said quickly. "Just some litter someone left behind."

Jonny looked like he wanted to ask more questions, but Henry gave him a look that said they had nothing else to say about it.

"Hmm," said Jonny, raising an eyebrow. "Well, then. I'll let you four explore the rest of the museum on your own." After that he walked away to chat with other visitors.

The children looked through the rest of the museum without Jonny, which was just as well. It seemed it was true that Fred Feriston had left very little behind. The most interesting thing the children found was a video from the local news at the time. It showed a young woman with braided brown hair being interviewed.

"Fred was very clever," the woman told the interviewer. "When we would hang out in the rafting shop, he would always bring crossword puzzles to pass the time. He loved word puzzles, and he was good with them too."

"He doesn't sound so bad," said Benny. "Grandfather likes crossword puzzles too."

The Aldens kept listening. "But there was always something mysterious about him. Sometimes I wondered if Fred was even his real name."

"So you think that the name 'Fred Feriston' might have been a part of his con too?" asked the interviewer.

This made the young woman upset. She furrowed her brow.

"He wasn't a con. He was a good person, and I believe he must have had a reason for taking the money," she said firmly. Then the video cut out and started over again.

While the interview with Fred's coworker played again, Violet walked back to the case with the handwritten letters. She was deep in thought.

"What is it, Violet?" Henry asked.

"Something about these letters seemed familiar," she said, trying to keep her voice down. "I didn't think much of it. But then that woman in the video said that Fred might have a different name. Now that I look at them again, doesn't the writing look like the writing in the journal I found?"

Henry nodded. "I think you're right!" He looked over at Jonny who was chatting with another visitor. "Take a photo. We'll compare it when we get back to the hotel."

After Violet took the photo, the Aldens said good-bye to Jonny and hurried out of the museum.

It was dark by the time the children returned to the hotel. There was a note at the front desk from Liz, saying she had gone on a walk, but she'd made a reservation for their dinner next-door at The Slippery Salmon. Before they went to the restaurant, Violet headed up to their room to get the journal from her pack. She wanted to look at it while they ate.

The Slippery Salmon was the only restaurant in town. It had heavy log tables and hanging lights that made it feel like an old tavern. The host found their reservation and showed them to their table. After they sat down, Jessie noticed the woman from the red kayak was sitting at a corner table reading a book.

"Yes, look at this!" Violet exclaimed. She was

comparing the front page of the journal with the photo of Fred Feriston's letters from the museum.

"The handwriting *is* the same," Henry said.

"If it is, that means Fred Feriston *wasn't* his real name," Violet said. "Just like the woman in the video thought. His real name was Christopher Francis!"

"We were sitting on a clue the whole time," said Henry. "Maybe there's something in the journal that explains why he did what he did."

Violet paged through the journal carefully. It had been well preserved in the plastic bag, despite being hidden behind a waterfall for many years. She turned all the way to the last entry and read it to herself.

"This entry says he planned to stay hidden until the search quieted down," she said. "He must mean the search after he left with the money. It says here, 'I feel bad about not telling my friends at the raft shop the truth, but I have something important I must do.'"

"Keep reading," Henry encouraged Violet. She nodded and read out loud.

"After I return to MT ST HELER and take care of

my final business there, I will continue on down the river."

"Final business?" Henry repeated. "What do you think that means?

"And what's Mt. St. Heler?" asked Jessie.

"Maybe he means Mount St. Helens!" Benny said loudly. He had seen that name on Jessie's map in their car ride to Hemlock. At Benny's outburst, everyone, including the woman from the red kayak sitting in the corner, looked up at them.

"Sorry. I got excited because I knew Mount St. Helens is a place in Washington," he said quietly.

"It is in Washington, but Mount St. Helens is a long ways from here," Jessie said. "I don't think Hemlock River goes all the way there. If he had made it that far, there's no telling how much farther he could have gone."

Henry nodded. "Something doesn't feel right about Mount St. Helens, anyway. For someone who was supposed to be clever, it seems strange he wouldn't remember the name of such an important place. Are you sure that's what he wrote, Violet?" he asked.

"Yes. It says here: MT ST HELER. It's definitely an R," Violet said.

Benny thought back to the video they saw in the museum. "That woman that knew him said Fred liked word puzzles," he said. "Maybe it's a puzzle!"

Violet nodded. The words did seem special. They were written in blocky capital letters, which were different from the smooth cursive of the rest of the journal. Next to the strange message, she wrote *Word puzzle?* She hoped they would find out what it meant soon.

CONTINUE TO PAGE 62

ON THE RIVER AGAIN

The next morning, the children woke up early. While they packed up and got ready to go, Jessie opened the window to let in the morning breeze. The birds were singing outside. It looked like it was going to be a beautiful day.

Liz was waiting for them in the hotel lobby.

"Ready for today's adventure?" she asked.

"Am I ever," Benny said. "What are we doing today?"

"Today we're rafting to one of my favorite stops on the river. I've got an afternoon activity planned for when we get there that I think you will all love."

As they made their way to the dock, Liz added, "The weather is wonderful, and the river is steady, so it should be a nice peaceful morning."

"What do you mean you want a refund?!" a voice yelled from the dock. It was Jonny, and the young couple on his tour did not look happy.

"So much for peaceful," Jessie muttered.

The unhappy man crossed his arms. "The Bandit River Tour stuff is fine, but after getting dumped in the rapids yesterday, we don't want to continue."

"We're going to stay here in town and go hiking instead," said the woman.

Jonny looked like he was going to yell some more. But when he saw the Aldens and others at the dock watching him, he forced a smile. "Why don't we go into town and figure something out," he said. "I have better things to do than bring unhappy customers down the river."

The group headed back to town, and the Aldens loaded up their raft.

"I can't imagine not wanting to be on the water on such a beautiful day," Violet said to her siblings.

"I can't either," said Jessie. "But I might feel different with Jonny as my guide. He knows a lot about Fred Feriston, but I'm not sure he knows that much about rafting."

Soon enough the Aldens were back on the water. If there were other rafters out, they must have been elsewhere. The group had the river all to themselves.

"Hey, Violet. Can I see that journal?" Jessie asked as they coasted downstream.

Violet was spending her time drawing in her notebook the scenes she saw along the river. She got the journal out and handed it to Jessie.

Jessie flipped through the pages, reading the entries to herself. They described the area being torn apart by logging and people Christopher knew getting hurt. Through it all, the logging companies didn't seem to care. The further Jessie got into the journal, the more upset the entries became.

I have to do something to change things—something big, one of the later entries ended. Jessie put the journal down. What had Fred planned to do? And how did taking money from other people help him do it?

"Heads up," Liz said.

The children looked where Liz was pointing. Along the side of the river was an old lumbermill. Nature had taken its course in the years since the building had gone out of use, with trees and brush growing all around it. A tall blue heron was perched on top of the roof, watching them with beady red eyes.

"That's one of the first lumbermills along Hemlock River," Liz said as they drifted by. "And one of the first to close down after James Green made a deal with the owner. Did you see the statue back in White-River Falls?"

"Yeah, the lumberjack and the businessman," Benny said.

"Right. The man with the ax is James Green. He'd been injured on the job when he worked as a logger. After that happened, he disappeared for a while. But when he came back, he was a changed man. Not only did he speak up for the workers, he also started an organization called Forest Friends, which fought for better forestry practices. The deal he made with the logging company was really a turning point in this area."

"That's what it said on the statue plaque," Jessie said. "It sounds like his organization was pretty important to the workers."

"Yes. And not just the workers." Liz pointed to the water. "See those fish?"

The children looked over the side of the raft. Swimming against the current were silvery fish.

"There are so many of them!" Violet gasped. "I didn't even notice!"

"Those are rainbow trout," Liz said. "The river is full of them. That wasn't the case back when all the logging was going on. But now that the logging has gone down, the fish have been able to bounce back. Not just trout, but salmon too. All swimming from the mountains down to the ocean," Liz continued.

"Is that what she's fishing for?" asked Henry. He nodded to a figure standing in the water downstream. As they got closer, the woman waved, and they recognized her as the one with the red kayak from the day before.

"Hey, Maggie," Liz called. "Catch anything?"

"Not with you shouting like that, I won't," Maggie said, but she was teasing.

Maggie waved them over. She held a long, thin fishing pole with a bright yellow line that dangled from the end.

"Is that a fly-fishing rod?" Henry asked.

"It sure is," said Maggie. "Are you kids enjoying your tour with Liz? Her tours are the best."

Everyone nodded.

"We've got a big surprise later," said Benny.

Maggie saw Henry's interest in her rod. "Well, I don't want to interrupt your plans. But I'd be happy to teach you to fly-fish for a little bit if you'd like."

"Oh, I don't know," Henry said. "Do we have time?"

"Our excursion will take most of the afternoon," said Liz. "But if you want to stop for a little bit, we can make it shorter. After all, it's your adventure!"

Henry glanced at his siblings. "What do you think?" he asked.

"It's up to you, Henry," Jessie said. "But we need to choose before we float past!"

IF THE ALDENS STOP AND FISH WITH MAGGIE,
GO TO PAGE 68.

IF THE ALDENS CONTINUE ONWARD,
GO TO PAGE 74.

A FISHY DETOUR

"Let's stop," Benny said. "Can you imagine the look on Grandfather's face if we tell him we went fly-fishing too?"

"We might even catch supper," said Jessie.

Benny's eyes got big. "I didn't even think of that! Now we have to do it."

Together they pulled the raft far enough onto the shore so it wouldn't float away.

"I've got an extra rod in my pack," Maggie said, wading out of the water to join them. "But only one, so you'll have to take turns."

"Henry can go first since he looks the most interested," Jessie suggested.

Henry found the rod among Maggie's things. Benny and Henry stood close while Maggie showed them how to put it together and thread the line.

"Where's the bobber?" Benny asked.

"There isn't one. That's what makes fly-fishing different," Henry said.

Maggie nodded. "Exactly. The idea with fly-fishing is that you cast the lure over the surface of the water instead of letting it sink," she explained.

Benny looked at the lure. It was green and orange but was shaped like a bug.

"Oh, I get it," he said. "It's like a fly that lands on the water! Fly-fishing."

Maggie smiled. "Exactly." She showed Henry how to cast the line. The lure didn't weigh much at all, so it was challenging to get it to fly out over the water. But after a few tries, Henry got the hang of it.

While Henry, Benny, and Maggie were fishing, Violet and Jessie grabbed some of their packs from the raft and had a snack under a tall cedar tree. They weren't too interested in fishing, but they were happy to relax.

At the sound of a truck engine, everyone looked up. Across the river, a road wound just above the shoreline. A familiar blue truck drove by.

"Bandit River Tours," Benny said from the river. He looked back to Liz. "Do you think Fred Feriston stopped here? Maybe he went fishing!"

Maggie snorted. "No, I don't think Fred would have stopped somewhere so close to the road. He was too smart for that," she said.

"Do you think Jonny will ever find Fred Feriston or figure out why he left with all the money?" Violet asked Maggie.

"Jonny? He doesn't care about what happened or where Fred went. All he cares about is his business," Maggie said.

Violet was surprised that she knew so much about Fred and Jonny. It seemed like she felt strongly about both of them. But before Violet could ask Maggie any more questions, Henry yelped and jerked on the fishing rod.

"I think I got one!" he called. The fish on the line splashed and leaped out of the water. Henry handed the rod to Benny, who stood next to him near the raft.

"Go on and reel it in, Benny!" he said.

"Okay!" Benny said. "This one looks big. I bet he'll make a great supper."

Benny struggled with the rod. He stuck out his tongue and turned the reel. "Come on, fishy."

But it seemed more like the fish was pulling Benny toward the water than the other way around.

"You can do it, Benny!" Violet cheered.

"I've got you now," Benny said, leaning back with the rod.

But just then the fish gave its own pull. Benny stumbled forward, right into their raft. As he tumbled in, the fish kept pulling on the line. Benny didn't let go of the rod, and the fish yanked the raft right into the river!

Maggie splashed into the water to catch the raft, but it was too late.

"Benny, let the fish go and paddle back to shore before you hit the current," Maggie called. But Benny was stubborn.

"I've almost got it!" he called as he floated down the river.

But the fish did not give up. It yanked and pulled,

even as Henry and Maggie told Benny to let it go. Finally, the fish flipped out of the water, came off of the hook, and darted away.

Benny was free from the fish, but he was well into the river now. He took his paddle and tried to move the raft back to the shore, but by himself, it wasn't enough.

"Now what?" he called. "The current is too strong!"

"Jump out and swim to shore!" Liz said. "Henry and I will get you."

With a splash, Benny jumped out of the raft. His life jacket helped him pop back up, and he swam toward shore. Henry ran into the water to get him. A minute later they were back on land, all wet but safe. The five of them and Maggie watched the raft float away.

"Well, I guess we'll be camping here tonight," said Liz.

THE END

TO FOLLOW ANOTHER PATH, GO TO PAGE 67.

ONWARD, UPWARD

"Let's keep going and get to our campsite," Henry said. "After all, Liz made plans, and I want to see what she has in store for us."

Liz grinned. "Good choice," she said.

They said good-bye to Maggie and paddled back into the current. After they'd traveled a ways down the river, Violet saw a flash of blue appear along the shoreline.

"Is that a vehicle?" she asked.

As they got closer, they could see a truck was parked on a road alongside the river—a familiar truck.

"What's Bandit River Tours doing here?" Jessie asked.

"Maybe Jonny decided to do something else

with his day now that his tour group canceled on him," said Henry. But if Jonny had driven down in the truck, he was nowhere in sight.

A good time later, Liz motioned for them to paddle to the shore, where there was a sandy beach. They pulled the raft all the way out of the water and looked around. Up the bank was a flat clearing with a stone circle in the middle. They'd made it to the campsite!

"Let's set up our tents and eat some lunch. Then we can leave for our excursion," Liz said.

The Aldens had plenty of experience setting up tents, although Benny needed some help with the collapsible poles. After their tents were up and their beds were made, they had a quick lunch.

"I wish we had some fish," said Benny.

"Oh Benny, who knows what would have happened if we had stopped," said Jessie. "You might not have caught anything."

"Benny, I have a feeling you are especially going to like our excursion," said Liz. She packed up their leftover food and pulled out a rope and pulley.

"What's that for?" asked Violet.

"Now that we're in the wild," Liz said. "We need to protect our food against curious critters."

She tossed the rope over a branch and used the pulley to lift the food pack. After the pack was high up in the air, Liz tied off the rope to the tree trunk and picked up a daypack.

"Is it time?" Benny asked. "For the special trip?"

Liz nodded. "This way."

She led the children down a narrow trail through the forest. Before long, the path got steeper. Higher and higher they went into the tree-covered hills. Jessie turned to look over her shoulder. She could see the tops of the hemlocks spreading out in the valley behind them.

When the group finally reached the top of their climb, the trees parted, revealing a sunny hill covered in fluffy bushes. From there, they could see far and wide across the valley below. The early evening light was so warm and golden that everyone stood for a moment to take it in.

"Is this the surprise?" Benny asked. He liked being so high up, but he sounded a little disappointed.

"Yes," Liz said. "But you haven't seen the best part yet. Do you recognize these bushes?"

Benny looked closer. The bushes were bright green with pale berries growing on them. He recognized them, and any disappointment went away. "Blueberries!"

Liz nodded. "Nothing used to be able to grow here. It was where the loggers kept their trucks. Now that they've moved, blueberries grow all over this hilltop. And I'll tell you, they're the best berries you'll taste in the state of Washington."

Liz had come prepared with four tin bowls for holding the berries. Everyone began filling their bowl with the juicy berries. Everyone except for Benny. He pulled them off the bushes and right into his mouth. Before long Benny's shirt was stained with purple blueberry juice.

"Worth it," he said, looking down at himself, and everyone laughed.

After they had all picked some berries, Violet spotted a steep hill that rose up above them. "Henry, can we go up there? I bet I could take some great pictures."

"Sure," said Henry. "I think we have time for another short hike."

"Wait a minute," Liz said. She rustled around in her daypack and finally pulled out an old folded map. "Take this. The way isn't too difficult, but there are a lot of footpaths in these woods. This should help you get there and back."

"Take care not to get lost," Jessie said.

"We will," said Henry. "And you make sure not to eat too much," he told Benny, who hadn't moved from his spot next to the blueberry bushes.

Henry and Violet headed off along the trail in the direction of the hill. Jessie took a seat next to Benny as he ate. She wished she had Christopher's journal to read, but they'd left it at the campsite, so she was happy to sit in the sun and relax.

After a while, Violet and Henry appeared on the hill above them.

"Better start on the way down," Liz called up to them. She looked up at the sky, which was getting gray. "We don't want to get caught out in the rain."

Henry nodded, and after Violet had taken some pictures, they started back down.

The sky continued to get darker. Jessie and Benny started to worry. "I wonder what's taking them," Jessie said.

"Yes. They should have been back by now," Liz agreed. "Those clouds don't look good. They've got rain in them, and they're going to make things darker much quicker."

As they were about to set out looking for Violet and Henry, there was a rustling in the bushes, and the two popped out. They looked a little frustrated.

"Sorry it took so long," Henry said. "When we saw that clouds were on the way, we tried to take a shortcut, but the trail led us a different way, and we had to turn around. It was the strangest thing."

"That does sound strange," said Jessie. Normally Henry was very good with maps.

Liz looked at the map. A frown stretched across her face.

"No wonder you had trouble. This map is almost twenty years old!" she said. "The trails must have changed. I've got to have a word with my dad for keeping such old stuff around. He insists that his old gear works just fine."

"Well, I'm glad you got back okay," said Jessie.

Benny looked up as a wet spot hit his forehead. The first drops of rain were beginning to fall, and it had suddenly gotten very dark as the heavy clouds rolled in.

Liz frowned.

"All right, maybe a change of plans," she said. "There's a hiking cabin nearby where we can wait out the storm."

"But what if the rain doesn't stop?" said Violet. "All our stuff is back at the campsite."

"The cabin will have some food and bunks in case we need to stay the night," said Liz. She looked down into the valley where their campsite was. "It could be dangerous to hike down in the dark, especially if the rocks get slippery. But what would you like to do?"

IF THE ALDENS GO TO THE HIKING CABIN,
GO TO PAGE 82.

IF THE ALDENS HEAD BACK TO CAMP,
GO TO PAGE 91.

THE HIKING CABIN

The rain came down harder. The children would soon be drenched. The thought of trying to get back down to the campsite was not a happy one.

"Let's find that cabin," Henry said.

Liz looked at the old map. It was getting quite dark now, so she shined her flashlight to see better. "Here," she said.

Henry looked where Liz was pointing. Above an icon of a little building were words that had been shortened to save space: FRST TRL SHELTER.

"First trail shelter?" he asked.

"Close," said Liz. "We're on the forest trail, and that is the forest trail shelter."

"But this map is old," said Jessie. "What if the shelter is not there?"

Liz motioned toward the trail. "This path is still maintained, so I'm sure the shelter will be maintained too," she said. "Still, I wouldn't expect too much."

"That's fine with us," said Henry. "Let's go."

The forest shelter was actually much closer than it had appeared on the map, and it was a good thing, because the rain was starting to come down hard. After a short trek, they could make out the shape of a small building shaped like the icon on the map. It looked old with a tattered log roof and an opening where the door should be.

"It's kind of spooky," Benny said as he looked into the shelter.

"It will beat sleeping in a tent in this rain," Liz said.

Once they were inside and Liz had lit some candles she'd found in the cabinets, the little cabin wasn't so bad. The floor was packed dirt, and there were a few wooden bunks with no mattresses. The rain dripped a little through the holes in the roof, but despite it all, the Aldens were happy to have a safe place out of the rain and wind.

"Actually, this reminds me of our boxcar," Benny said. The thought of that made him smile. "Do you remember the day we found the boxcar? We went blueberry picking that day too!"

Jessie grinned. She was looking through the cupboards.

"I remember. And guess what I've found?" she said, turning around with an old, dusty tablecloth.

"That brings back memories," Henry said with a laugh.

Liz started going through the cupboards too. Unlike the shelter itself, the cupboards had latching handles, probably to keep wild animals from using the shelter as a buffet. "There's some canned soup here somewhere. Our tin bowls should be fine to heat it in if I can find it."

While Jessie got a fire started in an old wood-burning stove, Henry, Violet, and Benny sat at the big wooden table. Liz found some cans of soup that hadn't quite expired, and together they had a little supper. While they ate, Jessie had a thought.

"Liz, can I see that old map again?" she asked.

"Sure," Liz said. She took out the map from her

bag. It had gotten damp from the rain, but it would dry out with time. The children looked it over as Jessie pointed at the spot where they were now, the place marked FRST TRL SHELTER.

"This is short for *forest trail shelter*, right?" she asked. "It got me thinking about that strange thing Violet read in the journal she found: MT ST HELER. I wonder if it's the same kind of thing."

Violet thought back to the journal and remembered where she'd left off. "That woman in the interview said Fred Feriston—or Christopher Francis—loved word games," she said.

Benny grabbed a stick from the wood pile. On the dirt floor, he used the stick to draw the letters from the journal. But Benny was still getting used to spelling, and some of the letters he wrote were out of order.

"Oops," he said when he noticed what he'd done. "Oh well, I've got an eraser right here!"

Benny was about to use his foot to spread dirt back over the letters he'd written.

"No, wait a minute, Benny," Violet said. "Everyone, look."

Race through White-Water Canyon

Benny stopped spreading the dirt and looked down at the letters he'd written: MT SHELTER.

"Shelter," Jessie said. "Mountain shelter! I just knew something was strange about that message."

"Christopher must have made his destination into a puzzle," said Henry. "So if someone found the journal, they still wouldn't be able to find him."

Benny looked sideways at the letters he'd written. "You mean I didn't jumble up the letters?"

Jessie smiled. "You unjumbled them," she said. "Fred was the one to jumble them up. He created what's called an anagram. It's a type of word puzzle."

"Just like you said, Violet," said Henry. "It was a puzzle after all!"

"So Fred wasn't going to Mount St. Helens; he was heading to a mountain shelter," said Violet. "That makes more sense."

Liz rubbed her chin. "There are many shelters on the mountains along the river," she said. "But he probably would have tried to go to one close to shore. I don't know of any of those."

Henry turned back to the map on the table. "You might not know of any *today*, but the one we're

looking for was around twenty years ago, just like this map."

"It might show us where the old cabins are!" said Liz. Then she chuckled. "Maybe my dad is right. Some old things are worth holding onto."

The five of them looked closely at the map. They searched the squiggly lines that represented hiking trails near the river.

"What about this one?" Violet said, pointing at an icon like the one for the forest trail shelter. "It's on a mountain."

Liz squinted. "Could be. I know for a fact that spot isn't on any of the tour maps I normally use," she said.

"This is exciting," Benny said. "Another clue!"

Liz laughed. "Yes, well. We'll have to wait until tomorrow to keep sleuthing. Tonight, the best thing we can do is get some sleep."

The children each took a bunk and used the extra clothes they had brought for pillows. It wasn't as comfortable as an air mattress would be, but with the warm stove and the gentle rain outside, the Aldens fell right asleep.

Race through White-Water Canyon

In the morning, the rain had cleared, and the sun was shining again. The children felt like they had made the right decision. Still, they were eager to make their way back to the campsite.

Without the slippery rain, the trek back down the mountain was no problem. But when they reached their campsite, there was a different kind of problem.

"Our packs!" Violet cried.

Their clothing packs were on the ground outside of their tents. The flaps were open, and their contents were strewn about. The food pack, which they had hung to keep away from bears, lay on the ground with the pulley and rope in a heap next to it.

Benny's eyes got wide. "Do you think bears did this?"

Liz took a look over their things. There was an unopened granola bar lying on the ground. "No, this wasn't animals. They'd never leave a delicious treat like this. In fact, I'm not really sure if anything at all is missing."

"There's one thing at least," said Violet, looking

through her clothing bag. "Christopher Francis's journal."

"Are you sure?" asked Jessie. "Maybe it's in the tent."

Before Jessie and Violet could go inside to look, Benny pointed toward the water. "Look!" he said.

A flash of red darted down the river. Someone in a red kayak was racing away from the campsite.

"Maggie?" Henry asked. "Do you think she could have done this?"

"The journal isn't in the tent either," Violet said after taking a look. "It's definitely missing."

Liz was relieved that all of their food and gear seemed to be intact. But she could tell that the missing journal meant a lot to Violet and that finding answers to the Fred Feriston mystery was important to all of them. In fact, she found herself wanting to know more too.

"Let's pack our things," Liz said. "If we hurry, we can still catch up!"

CONTINUE TO PAGE 96

JOURNEY THROUGH THE DARK

"Let's try to make it back to the campsite," Henry said. "We can set up a tarp and weather out the storm there. At least we'll be back with all our packs and the raft."

"All right, but we have to be very careful," Liz said. "Keep an eye on one another, and everyone stay close. Jessie, you're with Henry. Benny and Violet are with me. Let's go."

Liz had two flashlights. She handed one to Henry, who took up the rear, and she led the way with the other. The rain started to come down. Over time the drops grew. After about ten minutes tiny rivers streamed down the dirt trail. It was almost dark now, with the clouds and the trees of the forest keeping the setting sun's light out.

Race through White-Water Canyon

The path was difficult, especially in the dark. The children held on to trees to keep from slipping on the rocks, which were slick with rain. Finally, the slope leveled out. They were almost back to the campsite.

Suddenly, something rustled in the woods to the right of the path. From the back of the pack, Henry turned and pointed his flashlight toward the noise. He couldn't see anything move.

"Ouch!" Jessie called from in front of him.

Henry turned the flashlight back to the path, revealing an uneven, rocky trail. Without being able to see, Jessie had lost her footing and tripped. She was now sitting on the ground and wincing in pain.

"Jessie!" Henry cried. He knelt beside her. "I'm so sorry. Can you stand?"

Liz, Violet, and Benny had been a little ways down the trail and hurried back. Liz checked out Jessie's ankle.

"I think it's just twisted," she said. "We'll have to help you walk."

The Aldens helped Jessie up.

"I'm sorry I pointed the flashlight away," Henry said. "It's just that I heard something in the—"

Again there was a rustle coming from just off the path. Henry shined his light where the sound was coming from and slowly made his way over. A patch of brush shook a little.

"Maybe it's a bear," said Benny.

Henry called out, "Hey, bear!" He'd learned in his outdoors club that if he ever did come across a bear in the forest, it was best to let it know he was there. That way the animal wouldn't get surprised and attack.

Henry heard the rustle again, and a brown animal emerged from the brush. It wasn't big enough to be a bear. It wasn't even big enough to be a bear cub. Instead of being furry, it had spines up and down its back and a bushy tail.

"A porcupine!" Liz said.

"Well, Jessie, it could have been worse," said Benny. "You could have landed on that!"

The little critter waddled away into the brush, and the Aldens headed back on their way, with Henry and Liz helping Jessie along.

They managed to get back to camp without any more slipups, but Jessie was still in pain. She sat in the tent and tried to dry off while she rubbed her swelling ankle. After a little while, Liz came in.

"I just called my father," she said. "Judging by the swelling in that ankle, I think the safest thing is for us to go back to Hemlock. He'll meet us on the road in a little while."

Jessie sighed. She didn't want their adventure to be over, and she felt bad about interrupting Grandfather's fishing trip. But the way her ankle was feeling, she also couldn't imagine continuing on.

Liz was right. Stopping now was for the best.

THE END

TO FOLLOW ANOTHER PATH, GO TO PAGE 81.

RACE TO THE MOUNTAIN

The children quickly tore down their campsite and packed up their raft. Then they pulled on their life jackets and helped Liz push the raft back into the water. They'd have to organize their things later. Now they had to catch up to Maggie.

The group paddled hard. The current was steady and not too rough, and after a while Maggie's kayak came into view. As it did, the banks of the river rose up, and the valley became more like a canyon between two cliffs.

"We're in White-Water Canyon now," said Liz. "It's rockier here, so we'll need to pay extra attention."

Ahead, there was a split in the river, and like the first time, Maggie turned right.

Liz looked very serious when she addressed the Aldens.

"That way is Rockslide Creek," she said. "It's some of the toughest rapids in the area, especially at this time of year. I know you want to catch up to her, but it's a big risk. I don't know if we're ready for it."

"And the other way?" Jessie asked.

"That's the main route through White-Water Canyon. It will take longer, and it can still be tough, but we definitely have a better chance of staying in the raft," Liz said.

The children looked ahead to the split. They had a decision to make, and soon.

IF THE ALDENS GO DOWN ROCKSLIDE CREEK, GO TO PAGE 98.

IF THE ALDENS TAKE THE SAFER ROUTE THROUGH WHITE—WATER CANYON, GO TO PAGE 103.

THROUGH ROCKSLIDE CREEK

"Who else could have taken the journal?" Jessie said. "Maggie knew we had it back at The Slippery Salmon, and she keeps popping up at every turn."

"But why would she take it?" asked Violet.

"Only one way to find out," said Henry. "Liz, let's go after her. We're ready."

The other Aldens nodded in agreement.

"All right," said Liz. "But I need you all to pay very close attention. Here we go!"

Liz veered the raft right. Immediately the current picked up speed. Drops from the river sprayed in their faces as the raft crashed ahead, bouncing off rocks that jabbed out of the river like teeth.

At every turn Liz was ready. She called out

commands, and the children reacted. They had been in enough adventures to know that paying attention and listening to the expert were the best ways to get through a challenging situation. Liz had eyes like an eagle as she navigated them through the white water.

"Big drop. EVERYONE DOWN!" Liz yelled.

The children dove to the center of the raft as they went over the drop. Liz whooped with excitement as they fell. It was exhilarating!

The raft hit the water, and a wave washed over the front. For a moment it seemed like the raft might stay underwater, but a moment later, it shot back out, and they were on their way again.

Then, almost as quickly as they had sped up, the rapids calmed. Liz took her position again at the back of the raft. The Aldens sat up too. Big smiles spread across each of their faces.

"What a ride!" cheered Benny. "Just like a roller coaster!"

"Great job, everyone," Liz said. She was out of breath but was smiling bigger than any of them. Benny wasn't sure he had ever seen her so happy.

Then she squinted. Up ahead Maggie was still zipping away in her red kayak. They'd gained on her, but if they didn't hurry, they would lose her.

"Umm...what's that sound?" Jessie asked.

A high-pitched whining was coming from the raft near where Jessie was sitting. It sounded like air coming out of a balloon.

"Oh, shoot," Liz said. She bent over the side of the raft and groaned. "Come on, we need to paddle to shore. Quickly! There's a rip in the raft."

The group paddled as the raft deflated. In minutes the raft was nothing more than a rumpled pile of vinyl along the shoreline. A big hole had been torn in the side from one of the rocks they'd bumped into on the rapids.

"At least we're all safe," Jessie said.

"Yeah, but Maggie got away." Benny sounded glum.

The four of them looked up the river. There was no sign of Maggie or her red kayak. Benny was right. Wherever she was going, she would be getting there long before them, with plenty of time to escape.

They'd had an awesome adventure, but the mystery of the white-water bandit would go unsolved.

THE END

TO FOLLOW A DIFFERENT PATH, GO TO PAGE 97.

AROUND THE BEND

"We'll have to let her go, then," Henry said. "It's more important that we're all safe. We can't get to the bottom of any mysteries if we don't make it through the rapids."

"Good call," Liz said. She signaled, and they paddled left to keep the raft on the main river, leaving the dangerous Rockslide Creek behind. The group would have to find another way to figure out what Maggie was up to.

The river on the bend was level enough that Henry could take a break from paddling to look at the map. Even though it was outdated, it seemed to be coming in handy for their mystery.

"If this map is right, this part of the river curves around. It will meet up with Rockslide Creek on the other side," he said. "And guess what else? That's exactly where the hiking trail to the mountain shelter begins."

"That must be where Maggie's headed with Christopher Francis's journal," Violet said.

"We have to catch up to her," said Henry. He put the map away. "Let's paddle!"

They made good time on the bend of the river. It was a longer route, with a few rapids, but mostly the water was smooth, and they could focus on paddling.

When they came to the place where Rockslide Creek poured back into the main river, Violet gasped. On the left bank up ahead was the red kayak. It lay on its side, not quite out of the water. Water was sloshing up against it.

On the right side of the river, Henry noticed a single wooden docking post. "That's where the hiking trail to the mountain shelter is," he said.

"But where's Maggie?" Jessie asked. "Her kayak is tipped over on the wrong side of the river. What if she's in trouble?"

"I don't see her," said Henry. "Maybe she left

her kayak there to throw us off her trail? If she already headed up the trail, she could get to the shelter first."

"Oh, I don't know," Benny said, wringing his hands. "What should we do?"

IF THE ALDENS STOP TO CHECK OUT THE KAYAK, GO TO PAGE 106.

IF THE ALDENS GO UP THE MOUNTAIN, GO TO PAGE 110.

HELPING HAND

"Maggie loves that kayak," Liz said. "I don't think she would let it drift around like that just to fool someone."

"Let's go and make sure she's all right," Henry said.

When the group got closer, they could see a figure lying in the grass on the shoreline. It was Maggie. She was breathing heavily, catching her breath.

"Are you all right?" Henry asked. They pulled up the raft and ran to her.

Maggie looked startled to see them at first but then seemed relieved. "Yes, I'm fine. Just took a dunk in the river and scratched my arm on a rock. Those rapids are tough this time of year!"

Maggie sat up and looked at them kindly. "I

appreciate you stopping, but what are you all doing here? I would have thought you'd still be eating breakfast at this time, not out on the river."

The children looked at Maggie. She didn't seem to know anything about their ruined campsite or their missing journal or that they had been following her down the river.

"You mean you weren't running away from us?" Benny asked.

"Running away? Why would I do a thing like that?" Maggie asked with a funny smile.

"Someone took a journal I found," Violet said.

"You mean Fred's old journal?" Maggie asked. She explained, "I heard you all talking about that at the dock back in White-River Falls, and I meant to ask you about it. But why would I take it?"

"To find the way to the mountain shelter!" Benny said. Then he covered his mouth. "Oops."

Maggie laughed this time. "It's all right, little one," she said. "I already knew about the mountain shelter too. Or should I say, Mt. St. Heler. Which, by the way, gave me quite a chuckle back at The Slippery Salmon."

"But how were you able to figure it all out?" Liz asked.

Maggie gave a mysterious smile.

"Oh, you know what I've always said. Fred was very clever," she said.

"You knew him?" Violet asked. Then her eyes widened. There had been something familiar about Maggie that she couldn't put her finger on until now. "You were the woman in the interview that we saw back at the museum."

"Oh, yes. That was me. I worked at the rafting company when he was living in Hemlock," Maggie replied.

"Why didn't you ever say so?" Liz cried.

"You didn't ask," Maggie said. "He taught me how to kayak. Back then I didn't know anything about the river. Now I spend a lot of my time out here, hoping one day I'll find out where he went off to. Daydreaming, mostly," she added wistfully.

"But if you didn't take the journal, then that means someone else did," Henry said. He took out the old map from his pocket and looked across the river. It was definitely the place where the hiking trail to the mountain shelter began. "And if they've been able to figure out the secret behind the clue, they might be on their way up to the shelter right now. We should go."

"Are you sure you're all right?" Jessie asked. Liz helped Maggie to her feet.

"Yes. I just need some rest," said Maggie. She took a look at the map Henry was holding. "That's the right place, all right. But you should know that the mountain has changed since that map was made. The rockslide took out the path to the top."

Maggie took the map and pointed.

"Right about here is another trail. Take that one—it will get you up to the shelter safely," she said.

Henry nodded and tucked the map back into his pocket.

"Thanks," he said. "Now, let's find the real white-water bandit."

CONTINUE TO PAGE 114

ROCKSLIDE MOUNTAIN

"There's not much time," Henry said. "Liz, will you see if Maggie's on the left riverbank? The four of us will go up the trail. That way if Maggie needs help, you'll be there. But if she's already gone up the mountain, we might have a chance to catch up with her."

Liz glanced up the trail and hesitated. Then she nodded. "All right, but I'll be right behind you if I don't find Maggie."

They got the raft over to the dock pole, and the four Aldens climbed out.

"Be careful," she said. "That map you have is old. Who knows what you might run across!"

"We'll be careful," Jessie said.

The children left Liz as she paddled the raft

back across the river to where Maggie's kayak was. The trail up the mountain was overgrown with trees and shrubs, but they could still make it out with the help of Henry's old map.

Steadily the trail weaved its way up the slope. While it was a hard climb, Henry felt like the trail was leading them along the easiest way up.

"We're almost there," he called back to the others.

But when he turned around, he skidded to a stop. The trail had ended. In its place was a steep drop. Below they could see the boulders and rocks that gave Rockslide Creek its name.

"This wasn't on the map," Henry said.

"The rockslide must have wiped out the old trail," said Jessie.

"We can't go any farther," Violet said. "Let's turn back."

The Aldens doubled back and took another trail, then another. Each one they took seemed more and more overgrown. Until eventually Violet pointed through the trees. There was a building ahead, hidden among the hemlocks and cedars.

"The mountain shelter!" Benny said.

The children ran up the trail to the shelter, which was like a small cabin. Inside there was a single room with just enough furniture for one person to live comfortably.

Violet looked at the desk that sat in the corner under a window. One of the drawers was open, but nothing was inside.

"I think someone was just—" she started to say, but she was interrupted by a rumbling motor from behind the cabin.

The Aldens hurried outside just in time to see a cloud of dirt kick up behind a blue truck. On the side of the truck, the Aldens made out the words *Bandit River Tours*.

"Jonny!" Benny cried.

Jessie let out a groan. "So he's the one who stole the journal. He must have been following us down the river in his truck," she said.

The Aldens stood outside the empty mountain shelter as the dust from the Bandit River Tours truck settled. Benny gave a big sigh.

"I guess that's the end of that," Henry said.

"We found where Christopher Francis went after he escaped. But if he left anything in the cabin, it's gone for good now."

THE END

TO FOLLOW ANOTHER PATH, GO TO PAGE 105.

THE MOUNTAIN SHELTER

"I wonder what we'll find in the mountain shelter," Benny wondered aloud as they hiked. "Money? Another clue?"

"It's so out of the way," Jessie said. "It was probably the perfect hideaway."

"Here's where Maggie said we should turn off the path to go around the rockslide," Henry said, looking at the map. The Aldens left the main trail and hiked into the woods.

Maggie's directions were good. Even though the brush was thick, after a few minutes, the children had made it through. Ahead they could see the shape of a building through the trees. It was an old cabin, much sturdier looking than the forest shelter. Inside they found a table, two chairs, one bunk, and a desk.

"Look at this," Violet said as she inspected the desk. There was an envelope. The four children gathered around.

"Should we open it?" Benny asked. "You're not supposed to open other peoples' mail."

"That's true, but I think this was left for us," Jessie said. "Or maybe not us, specifically, but the people who found it. Look what it says on the envelope."

"'To any whose path brings them here,'" Violet read out loud. "That's us, I guess!"

"Give it a read," Henry suggested.

Violet took out the letter and unfolded it. She read it slowly, so they could all hear.

To any whose path brings them here:

You have probably arrived here after following the legend of Fred Feriston. I regret to inform you that you will not find any money here. However, I hope that as his friend I can offer a greater reward: the truth.

Several years ago I was badly injured while working at the White-River Sawmill. Despite this, the owners of the sawmill refused to make changes to how the sawmill was run. In fact, they did the opposite; they fired me and made it so I couldn't work in Hemlock or White-River Falls again. With my injury I found it difficult to travel elsewhere, and so I ended up in a very bad predicament.

That's when I met Christopher, or as you have probably come to know him, Fred. He had worked in the lumbermill for a short time. But when he saw what had happened to me, he decided he could no longer work for the company. He quit, and knowing I had nowhere else to go, he brought me here to stay while I recovered.

Christopher came to visit me, and we talked about what the logging companies were doing. We imagined how great it would be if the wilderness wasn't logged but allowed to grow and be managed properly—if people were friends to the forest. So we came up with a plan. As soon as I got better, we planned to get to work. But my recovery was slow.

By that time, his name had become connected with mine, so he used a different name, Fred Feriston. He raised money, not for his grandmother, but for me. That was when things started to go wrong. People started to suspect that Fred was keeping the money.

He became a wanted man, and he had to leave the area forever. But I moved forward with our work. When I had fully recovered, I used the money he had gathered to start Forest Friends, the organization that began right in this very cabin. And even though he is gone now, I hope that someday everyone will know the truth: that Fred Feriston was not a criminal but the first of many Forest Friends.

Sincerely,

James Green

"I can't believe this," said a man's voice from behind them. The children turned to see Jonny standing in the doorway. He had heard the whole letter.

Jonny sighed and rubbed his forehead, sitting down heavily in one of the chairs at the table. As he did, he dropped something onto the table with a heavy *thump*. It was the journal Violet had found behind the waterfall.

"The journal! You're the one who took it," Benny said.

"Why?" asked Henry.

"I'd heard rumors Fred had a journal like this,

with all his secrets," Jonny said. "When I learned that you children might have found it, I had to know what it said. But now that I know, I wish I hadn't found out. This is going to be terrible for my business."

More footsteps came up the path outside. A moment later Liz came in. She looked around at the Aldens, the letter Violet was holding, Jonny, and the journal on the table.

"What's going to be terrible for your business?" Liz asked, raising a brow.

"Fred Feriston was the first Forest Friend!" Benny said. "He wasn't a bandit at all. He used the money to help James Green, the lumberjack."

"And because of that," said Violet, "the logging companies made agreements to make things better for the workers and for the forest."

"This is awful," Jonny groaned. "I can't tell that story."

"Why not?" Jessie asked. "The people of Hemlock helped Fred Feriston. He helped his friend James Green. And James Green and the Forest Friends changed the whole valley for the

better. Right down to the rainbow trout, the blueberries, and the bald eagles. I think a lot of people would want to hear that story."

"With the added bonus that it's the truth," Liz remarked.

"No, that's not what I mean," Jonny said. "Telling the bandit story is the only thing I'm good at. It's the only reason people come to my tours! Every time I take people down the river in the raft, they end up in the water. I don't know the first thing about trout or blueberries or being a forest friend."

Jonny put his head in his hands.

"Luckily, you know someone who might be able to help with that," Jessie said, looking at Liz. "If she wanted to."

"And if you apologized," Henry added.

Jonny frowned. He turned to Liz and gave a big sigh.

"You're right. I'm sorry I've been such a jerk. About all this Bandit River stuff, and making fun of how you and your dad run your business. I leaned into the whole Fred Feriston bandit thing. But turns out he was more like you and your dad."

Jonny hung his head. "In the end there was only one bandit in town...me. I was making money off of a lie. I hope you'll let me try and make it up to you."

Liz sighed. For once it seemed like Jonny was being genuine and honest. And she *could* use some tips on attracting new customers and using social media. Jonny was good at that.

"I'd like that, Jonny..." said Liz. "But it can wait. Maggie is waiting for us down at the river. And she will definitely want to hear what we've found."

"Oh. Hmm...Do you think we should take a selfie before we go?" Jonny said. "To commemorate the occasion? You know. Hashtag-Fred-Feriston-was-Framed?" He winked, making sure they knew it was a joke.

Liz looked unsure at first, but then she saw the look on Benny's face.

"Can we, please?" he asked. "I want a picture to show Grandfather."

Jonny had already taken out his phone. He gathered everyone close. At first Liz didn't want to join in. But after Jessie made room and waved her over, she gave in. She stood next to Jessie and smiled into the camera.

"All right. Just one," she said. "Everyone say... forest friends!"

"Forest friends!"

After Jonny took the picture, the Aldens got ready to leave. As they left the old cabin behind them and headed down the trail, Violet thought of something.

"Forest friend," she said, laughing quietly at one last puzzle that Fred had left behind. "If you mix up the letters, they spell out Fred Feriston."

Liz chuckled at the thought. Violet was right.

"Well, in the words of someone who knew him well: Fred *was* very clever," Liz said.

And with that they continued down to the river to tell the true story of Fred Feriston to the one person who deserved to hear it the most.

THE END

Check out the other Boxcar Children Interactive Mysteries!

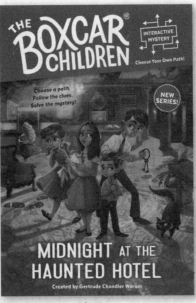

978-0-8075-2850-1 · US $6.99

The Boxcar Children investigate strange events at a hotel that some people say is haunted, and it seems like every room holds a new surprise.

978-0-8075-2860-0 · US $6.99

The Aldens put their sleuthing skills to the test in a spy competition put on by a famous author. Can you help them take the top prize?

978-0-8075-2862-4 · US $6.99

On a train tour of the Southwest, someone is bringing the lawless days of the Old West to life. Can you help the Aldens find out who is behind the trouble?

THE BOXCAR CHILDREN®

GREAT ADVENTURE

An Exciting 5-Book Miniseries

**Henry, Jessie, Violet, and Benny Alden
are on a secret mission that takes
them around the world.**

When Violet finds a turtle statue that nobody's seen
before in an old trunk at home, the children are on the
case. The clue turns out to be an invitation to the
Reddimus Society, a secret guild dedicated to returning
lost treasures to where they belong.

Now the Aldens must take the statue and six mysterious
boxes across the country to deliver them safely—and keep
them out of the hands of the Reddimus Society's enemies.
It's just the beginning of
the Boxcar Children's
most amazing
adventure yet.

**JOURNEY ON A
RUNAWAY TRAIN**
Created by Gertrude Chandler Warner

HC 978-0-8075-0695-0
PB 978-0-8075-0696-7

**THE CLUE IN THE
PAPYRUS SCROLL**
Created by Gertrude Chandler Warner

HC 978-0-8075-0698-1
PB 978-0-8075-0699-8

**THE DETOUR OF
THE ELEPHANTS**
Created by Gertrude Chandler Warner

HC 978-0-8075-0684-4
PB 978-0-8075-0685-1

**THE SHACKLETON
SABOTAGE**
Created by Gertrude Chandler Warner

HC 978-0-8075-0687-5
PB 978-0-8075-0688-2

**THE KHIPU AND
THE FINAL KEY**
Created by Gertrude Chandler Warner

HC 978-0-8075-0681-3
PB 978-0-8075-0682-0

**THE COMPLETE
FIVE-BOOK MINISERIES**
Created by Gertrude Chandler Warner

Also available as a boxed set
978-0-8075-0693-6 • $34.95

Don't miss the next two books in the classic Boxcar Children series!

THE BOXCAR CHILDREN®

BOOK 159

CREATED BY
GERTRUDE CHANDLER WARNER

Who is sabotaging
the honey harvest?

THE
BEEKEEPER MYSTERY

HC 978-0-8075-0823-7 · US $12.99
PB 978-0-8075-0824-4 · US $6.99

Add to Your
Boxcar Children Collection
with New Books and Sets!

The first sixteen books are now available in
four individual boxed sets.

978-0-8075-0854-1 · US $24.99

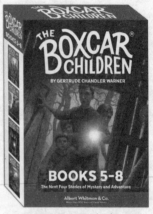

978-0-8075-0857-2 · US $24.99

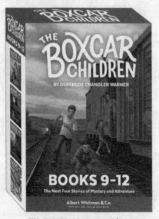

978-0-8075-0840-4 · US $24.99

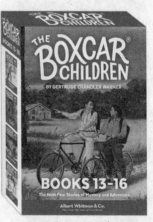

978-0-8075-0834-3 · US $24.99

Look out for
The Boxcar Children® DVDs!

The Boxcar Children and *Surprise Island* animated movie adaptations are both available on DVD, featuring Martin Sheen and J.K. Simmons.

Introducing The Boxcar Children®
Educational Augmented Reality App

Watch and listen to your favorite Alden characters as they spring from the pages to act out scenes, ask questions, and encourage a love of reading. The app works with any paperback or hardcover copy of *The Boxcar Children,* the first book in the series, printed after 1942.

Introducing The Boxcar Children® Early Readers

Adapted from the beloved chapter books, these new early readers allow kids to begin reading with the stories that started it all.

THE BOXCAR CHILDREN
HC 978-0-8075-0839-8 · US $12.99
PB 978-0-8075-0835-0 · US $4.99

SURPRISE ISLAND
HC 978-0-8075-7675-5 · US $12.99
PB 978-0-8075-7679-3 · US $4.99

THE YELLOW HOUSE MYSTERY
HC 978-0-8075-9367-7 · US $12.99
PB 978-0-8075-9370-7 · US $4.99

MYSTERY RANCH
HC 978-0-8075-5402-9 · US $12.99
PB 978-0-8075-5435-7 · US $4.99

MIKE'S MYSTERY
HC 978-0-8075-5142-4 · US $12.99
PB 978-0-8075-5139-4 · US $4.99

BLUE BAY MYSTERY
HC 978-0-8075-0795-7 · US $12.99
PB 978-0-8075-0800-8 · US $4.99

THE WOODSHED MYSTERY
HC 978-0-8075-9210-6 · US $12.99
PB 978-0-8075-9216-8 · US $4.99

THE LIGHTHOUSE MYSTERY
HC 978-0-8075-4548-5 · US $12.99
PB 978-0-8075-4552-2 · US $4.99

NEW!
The Boxcar Children®
DVD and Book Set

This set includes Gertrude Chandler Warner's classic chapter book in paperback as well as the animated movie adaptation featuring Martin Sheen, J.K. Simmons, Joey King, Jadon Sand, Mackenzie Foy, and Zachary Gordon.

978-0-8075-0928-9 · US $17.99

The Boxcar Children, Fully Illustrated

This fully illustrated edition celebrates Gertrude Chandler Warner's timeless story. Featuring all-new full-color artwork as well as an afterword about the author, the history of the book, and The Boxcar Children® legacy, this volume will be treasured by first-time readers and longtime fans alike.

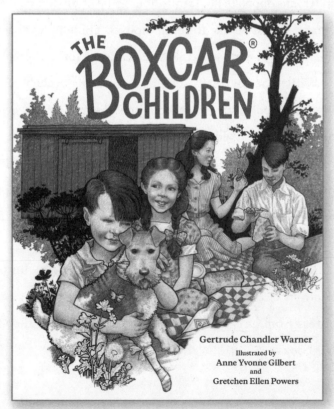

Gertrude Chandler Warner

Illustrated by
Anne Yvonne Gilbert
and
Gretchen Ellen Powers

978-0-8075-0925-8 · US $34.99

GERTRUDE CHANDLER WARNER discovered when she was teaching that many readers who like an exciting story could find no books that were both easy and fun to read. She decided to try to meet this need, and her first book, *The Boxcar Children*, quickly proved she had succeeded.

Miss Warner drew on her own experiences to write the mystery. As a child she spent hours watching trains go by on the tracks opposite her family home. She often dreamed about what it would be like to set up housekeeping in a caboose or freight car—the situation the Alden children find themselves in.

While the mystery element is central to each of Miss Warner's books, she never thought of them as strictly juvenile mysteries. She liked to stress the Aldens' independence and resourcefulness and their solid New England devotion to using up and making do. The Aldens go about most of their adventures with as little adult supervision as possible— something else that delights young readers.

Miss Warner lived in Putnam, Connecticut, until her death in 1979. During her lifetime, she received hundreds of letters from girls and boys telling her how much they liked her books.